S0-CAA-163

CHESTERFIELD COUNTY PUBLIC LIBRARY
CHESTERFIELD, VA

THE SMURF REPORTER

Peyo

THE SMURF REP⚬RTER

A *SMURFS* GRAPHIC NOVEL BY *Peyo*

WITH THE COLLABORATION OF
LUC PARTHOENS AND THIERRY CULLIFORD – SCRIPT
LUDO BORECKI – ART
NINE AND JOSÉ GRANDMONT – COLOR

PAPERCUT Z ™
NEW YORK

SMURFS GRAPHIC NOVELS AVAILABLE FROM **PAPERCUTZ**™

THE SMURFS graphic novels are available in paperback for $5.99 each and in hardcover for $10.99 each, except for THE SMURFS #21–#23, and THE VILLAGE BEHIND THE WALL, which are $7.99 in paperback and $12.99 in hardcover, at booksellers everywhere. You can also order online at papercutz.com. Or call 1-800-886-1223, Monday through Friday, 9 – 5 EST. MC, Visa, and AmEx accepted. To order by mail, please add $4.00 for postage and handling for first book ordered, $1.00 for each additional book and make check payable to NBM Publishing. Send to: Papercutz, 160 Broadway, Suite 700, East Wing, New York, NY 10038.

THE SMURFS graphic novels are also available digitally wherever e-books are sold.

PAPERCUTZ.COM

THE SMURF REPORTER

SMURF™ © Peyo - 2019 - Licensed through Lafig Belgium - www.smurf.com
English translation copyright © 2019 by Papercutz.
All rights reserved.

"The Smurf Reporter"
  BY PEYO
  WITH THE COLLABORATION OF
  LUC PARTHOENS AND THIERRY CULLIFORD FOR THE SCRIPT,
  LUDO BORECKI FOR ARTWORK,
  NINE AND JOSÉ GRANDMONT FOR COLORS.

"The Flute Smurfers"
  BY PEYO
  WITH THE COLLABORATION OF
  LUC PARTHOENS AND THIERRY CULLIFORD FOR THE SCRIPT,
  JEROEN DE CONINCK FOR ARTWORK,
  NINE CULLIFORD FOR COLORS.

Joe Johnson, *SMURFLATIONS*
Bryan Senka, *LETTERING SMURF*
Matt. Murray, *SMURF CONSULTANT*
Dawn Guzzo, *SMURFIC DESIGN*
Jeff Whitman, *ASSISTANT MANAGING SMURF*
Jim Salicrup, *SMURF-IN-CHIEF*

HARDCOVER EDITION ISBN: 978-1-6299-1851-8

PRINTED IN CHINA JANUARY 2019

Papercutz books may be purchased for business or promotional use. For information on bulk purchases please contact Macmillan Corporate and Premium Sales Department at (800) 221-7945 x5442.

DISTRIBUTED BY MACMILLAN
FIRST PAPERCUTZ PRINTING

Among all the Smurfs, there's one who loves to observe and learn. He scrupulously takes note of everything in his little pad. Here's his story...

That day...

Rhaaa! Stupid fishing line! It does the same thing every time!

HEY! LOOK...

!

EEEEEE

POC

SPLASH

Quack?

HEE HEE HEE! I'd better not stick around! Fisher Smurf would get annoyed at being seen...

Later...

?

So, Fisher Smurf? You've done smurfed in again, for smurf's sake?!

!

© Peyo

1

Ah, careful now. It's not at all what you think!

I'd been smurfing for a good while when CRACK! I hook something! HUP! I jump onto my two feet to smurf it out of the water, but ZIP! I slip and PLOOF! I smurf into the water...

Otherwise, believe me, I'd have smurfed one this big!

Well then...

I promise you, he told me himself he'd had to smurf for hours! It was this big!

According to Farmer Smurf, it was enormous, practically a monster! Can you imagine? What courage!

--A monster with enormous smurfs that tried to smurf him alive!

Soon, all of Smurf Village knew about it.

The monster had smurfs like that, it seems.

Could be he saved the village...

He's a hero!

Me, I don't like zeroes!

What's this I hear? Fisher Smurf's a hero? Ha! Ha! Ha! You must be joking?!

It's true! He defeated a monster trying to drag him to the bottom of the pond to smurf him alive!

Is he the one who told you that?

© Peyo

6

Uh...well...he's the one who told me he knew someone who saw it...

He's the one who started this story!

All I did was resmurf what Jokey Smurf told me...

He's the one who told me!

Me?! It wasn't you?

I don't know what you're smurfing about...

Anyhow, you all know full well there's never been a monster in the pond!

Hey, that's right!

I hadn't thought of that...

It's too bad, I liked the monster story...

Yeah, anyhow, what a bruiser that Fisher Smurf is!

Did you see that, Papa Smurf? They let themselves be smurfed by that ridiculous story!

What do you expect, it's a lack of information! And word of mouth does the rest...

But that's unthinkable nowadays, Papa Smurf! The Smurfs are entitled to correct information!

They have a right to know!

That's true! I'm smurfing you the mission of keeping the Smurfs correctly informed!

© Peyo

Thanks, Papa Smurf! I won't let you down!

3

The Smurf immediately sets out in search of stories...

BONK
BONK

...jotting down everything in his little pad...

And the next day...

Hey, what are you smurfing?

It's today's news! Everything that smurfed in the village yesterday is written there.

Did you see, Farmer Smurf? It's the news...

?

Listen to this: "Yesterday, Brainy Smurf was in for a rough time after lecturing Harmony Smurf..."

?

Ha! Ha! Good ol' Brainy Smurf, yep!

"...And Lazy Smurf slept all afternoon under the chestnut tree"?!

What the smurf! And I'd smurfed him three hazelnuts so he'd cut my logs! He's going to hear about this!

I'm sure this idea will help the Smurfs understand each other better...

© Peyo

4

8

Later...

I'm going to see if my news reports were successful...

Hey, you! Have you seen the latest news? What did you think of it?

?

Oh, yeah, that stuff there on the billboard...Nah! It was too crowded in front of it, so...

Bah! A Smurf who's probably uninterested... maybe even an idiot! He's got that look about him...

Hello, Handy Smurf! Did you read the billboard with the news?

?

Sorry, but I don't have time to go over there! That's all good and fine, but I'm working!

!

Hmmm! He's right! The Smurfs don't have time to go read the news...

Well then, the news will come to them!

That evening...

I'm going to smurf all the news onto sheets that I'll hand out and--

NOK NOK NOK

?

Are you the one who wrote I smurfed a nap all afternoon long yesterday? Because of you, I got my rear end smurfed by Hefty Smurf...

Sorry, Lazy Smurf, I'm just reporting objectively what I saw...

⇒Pfff!⇐ "Reporter" Smurf, right!

© Peyo

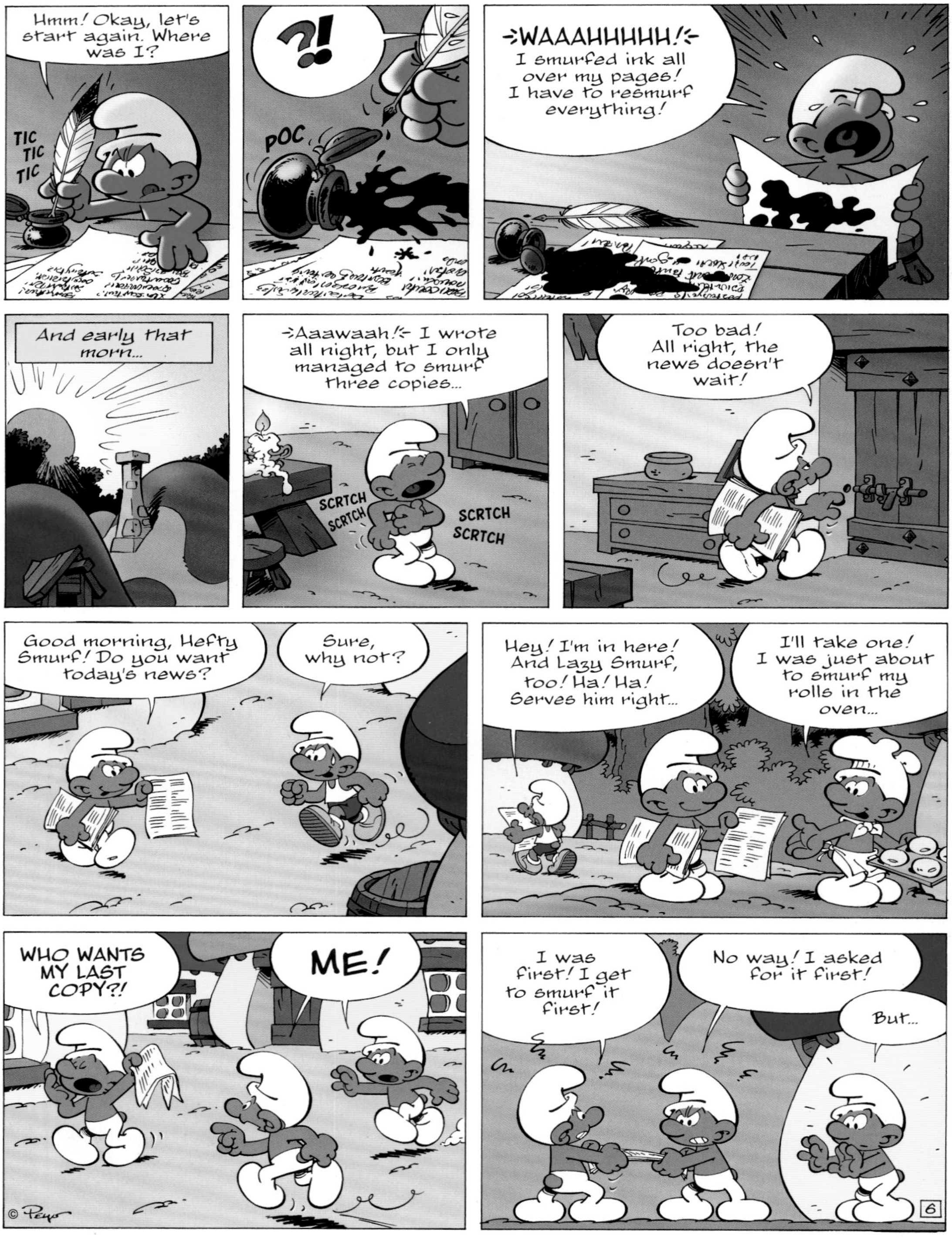
Hmm! Okay, let's start again. Where was I?
TIC TIC TIC
?!
POC
WAAAHHHHH! I smurfed ink all over my pages! I have to resmurf everything!
And early that morn...
Aaawaah! I wrote all night, but I only managed to smurf three copies...
SCRTCH SCRTCH
SCRTCH SCRTCH
Too bad! All right, the news doesn't wait!
Good morning, Hefty Smurf! Do you want today's news?
Sure, why not?
Hey! I'm in here! And Lazy Smurf, too! Ha! Ha! Serves him right...
I'll take one! I was just about to smurf my rolls in the oven...
WHO WANTS MY LAST COPY?!
ME!
I was first! I get to smurf it first!
No way! I asked for it first!
But...
6
© Peyo

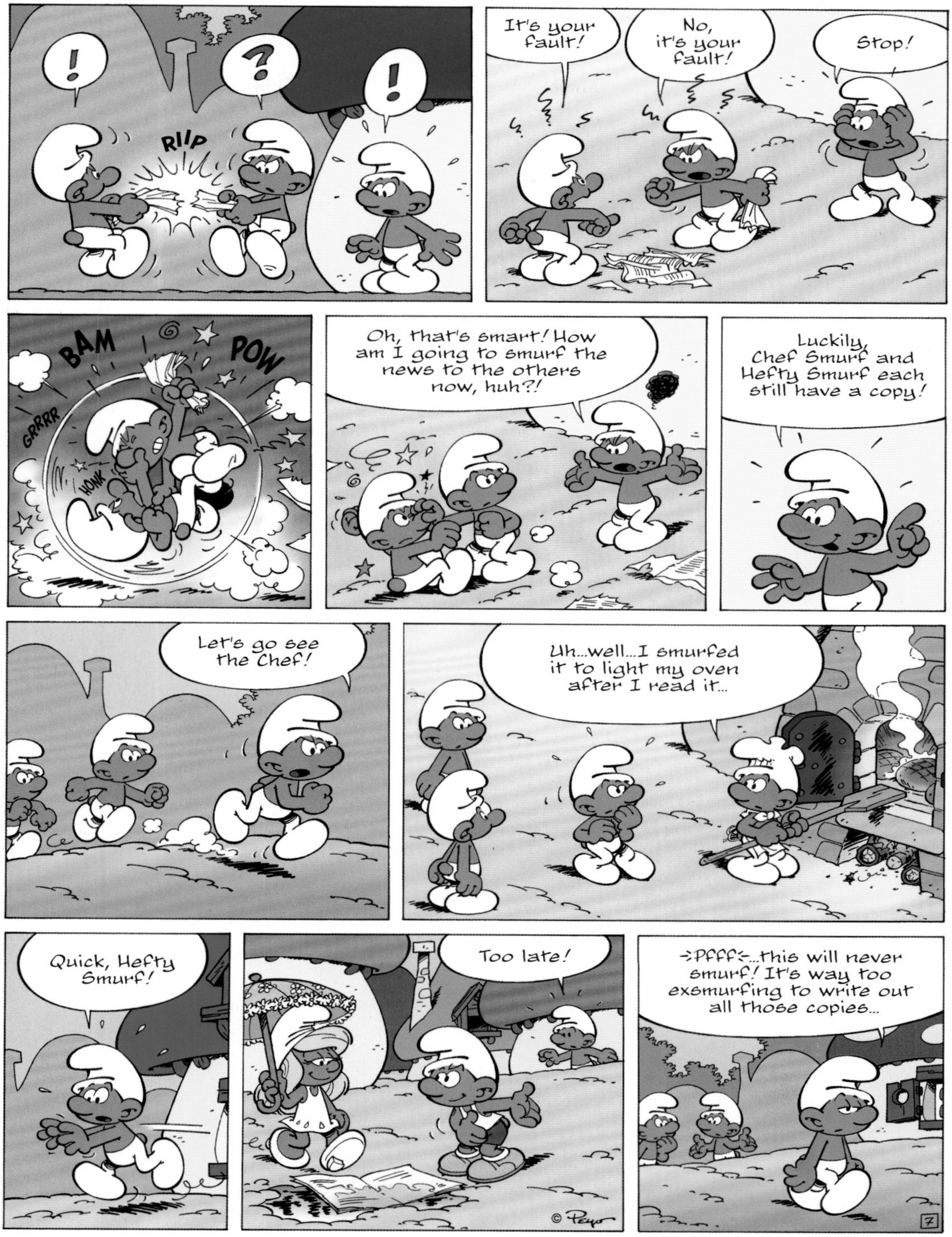
!
?
!
RIIP
It's your fault!
No, it's your fault!
Stop!
BAM
POW
GRRRR
HONK
Oh, that's smart! How am I going to smurf the news to the others now, huh?!
Luckily, Chef Smurf and Hefty Smurf each still have a copy!
Let's go see the Chef!
Uh...well...I smurfed it to light my oven after I read it...
Quick, Hefty Smurf!
Too late!
© Peyo
-Pfff-...this will never smurf! It's way too exsmurfing to write out all those copies...
7

Hello! Hey, you don't look too smurfy...

Bah!

Uh...Handy Smurf, you got a minute?

Soon after...

What?! A machine that writes for you and makes several copies?! Ha! Ha! Ha!

Come on, be serious, that's crazy! The one to smurf that machine hasn't been born yet!

→Bfff!← It's no big deal... I should've known!

→Tsk←... Why do they always think I can solve all their problems by smurfing a machine?!

Hello, Baby Smurf! Are you having fun in the sand?

Ga!

GAAAAA!

?

Huh?! Can I see what you smurfed there?!

8

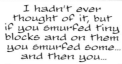

Do you see, Baby Smurf? The shapes carved on the blocks are smurfing a reverse image in the sand! That's smurfly interesting, don't you think?

?

I hadn't ever thought of it, but if you smurfed tiny blocks and on them you smurfed some... and then you...

Ga...

Why yes, of course! **SMURFREKA!**

Thanks, Baby!

?

SMACK

NOK NOK

Hey! Whatcha Smurf!

? A ? C ?

≥WAAAAAH≤

HEY! YO! WAIT UP!

?

I saw Baby smurfing with his blocks... and the prints on the sand...And the shapes... Then, I told myself--

So, in short, I think I can smurf your machine!

?

TAP TAP

© Peyo 9

13

Handy Smurf got to work right away...

DZEEEEEEEEE VRR RRR

CLANG BLONG POW OWW!

And soon...

Most of all, don't open your eyes till I smurf you to!

Well? What do you say?

SCTCH SCTCH

Wow! And... uh, how does it smurf?

Do you remember Baby Smurf's blocks? I asked Sculptor Smurf to smurf me some tiny ones with all the letters of the alphabet...

You smurf these letters on a composing stick to make sentences in reverse...

Why in reverse?

Because it won't smurf otherwise! Look, now I stick it on a plate and smurf ink all over it.

PLOSH PLOSH

Next, you place a sheet of paper underneath, you smurf everything under the press and-- ⇒UNNNN⇐...

?

© Peyo

10

14

And abracadabra! The text is printed in the right direction! And you can reprint it as many times as you like!

You see, it smurfs.

Handy Smurf, you're a genius! I'm sure people will still be talking about this invention for thousands of years!

Let's not exaggerate! Maybe for a few centuries...

That being said, it looks smurfly hard to go to press! I'll have to smurf someone to help me...

Oh, yeah! I really encourage you to do so!

Handy Smurf, I need your help!

?

Yum... ⇒Crunch!⇐ I've smurfed my nutcracker again!

Of course, Greedy Smurf. I've already told you those hazelnuts were way too big!

Hey!? Wha' tha' thing?

?

CHOMP CRUNCH

It's the first printing press, Greedy Smurf! What do you think?

Looks like a huge nut-cracker!

YUM CRUNCH

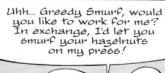

Uhh... Greedy Smurf, would you like to work for me? In exchange, I'd let you smurf your hazelnuts on my press!

?

Mmm... sure, why not? What do I have to smurf?

CHOMP CHOMP

© Peyo

11

15

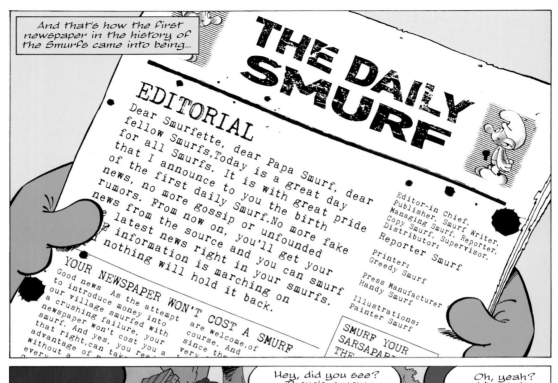

And that's how the first newspaper in the history of the Smurfs came into being...

THE DAILY SMURF

EDITORIAL

Dear Smurfette, dear Papa Smurf, dear fellow Smurfs,Today is a great day for all Smurfs. It is with great pride that I announce to you the birth of the first daily Smurf.No more fake news, no more gossip or unfounded rumors. From now on, you'll get your news from the source and you can smurf the latest news right in your smurfs. information is marching on nothing will hold it back.

YOUR NEWSPAPER WON'T COST A SMURF

Good news As the attempt to introduce money into our village smurfed with a crushing failure, your newspaper won't cost you a smurf. And yes, you read that right,can you rea advantage of n without a

are welcome,of course. And since the very the

Editor-in Chief, Writer, Publisher, Smurf Reporter, Managing Smurf, Reporter, Copy Smurf, Supervisor, Distributor:
Reporter Smurf

Printer:
Greedy Smurf

Press Manufacturer
Handy Smurf

Illustrations:
Painter Smurf

SMURF YOUR
SARSAPAR
THE

Hey, did you see? There's a new newspaper!

Oh, yeah? What's it about?

At the press... ⇒Arrgh!⇐ Greedy Smurf, you could at least clean the press before printing! These typos don't fix themselves!

! SMAK YUM CRUNCH

Bravo, Reporter Smurf, congratulations! Excellent idea...Hmm... that I might have had myself!!

?

© Peyo 12

16

That said, I caught a few unacceptable mistakes! That's why I'm nominating myself to be smurf editor of "The Daily Smurf"...

In addition, that will let us smurf my quotations on the front page every day, because a great newspaper owes it to itself to--

Brainy Smurf, your quotes are welcome, but it's my newspaper!

Reporter Smurf is right. You already bore us to death without us also having to read your nonsense every day in the newspaper!

OH!

And if you don't smurf it, you'll end up in tomorrow's newspaper, but not the way you were thinking!

What do you mean by that?

?

CRR

Hefty Smurf is right! You can't imagine all the accidents that could happen at a press!

GULP

CRRRRRRAC

I'm going to tell Papa Smurf!

Yeah, right...

Ha! Ha! Ha! Thanks, Hefty Smurf!

Hey, what's this I hear? There won't be anymore stories where Brainy Smurf gets some knocks on his smurf?!

It's because I have big plans for my newspaper! It must become THE ultimate authority on any subject! And for that, I must raise the level of my articles!

?

© Peyo

13

That's all good and fine! But what will I smurf?

I'm out of work now that the newspaper announces everything instead of me!

Don't worry, Drummer Smurf! You're exactly the Smurf I need!

Here, go hand out the newspapers! That way, you'll continue smurfing the news, and I'll have all my time for smurfing my reports!

Reporter Smurf immediately starts beating the bushes...

Is this your new style, Painter Smurf? Would you talk to me about it?

Well... I tried to smurf the whole quintessence of form to smurf the very expression of the subject! You understand? It's a question of lines of force!

Not so fast, not so fast!

SCRITCH SCRATCH

SPLOTCH

Later...

THE DAILY SMURF

PAINTER SMURF'S NEW TRENDS

Painter Smurf tells us: "I tried to smurf the whole quintessence of form to smurf the very expression of the

Unfortunately, the Smurfs don't show much interest...

I don't get it!

Bah! I preferred it when it was stories where Brainy Smurf got smacked!

The newspaper is interesting, don't you think? I couldn't have smurfed better!

→Nyyy!← I'm going to tell Papa Smurf!

© Peyo

14

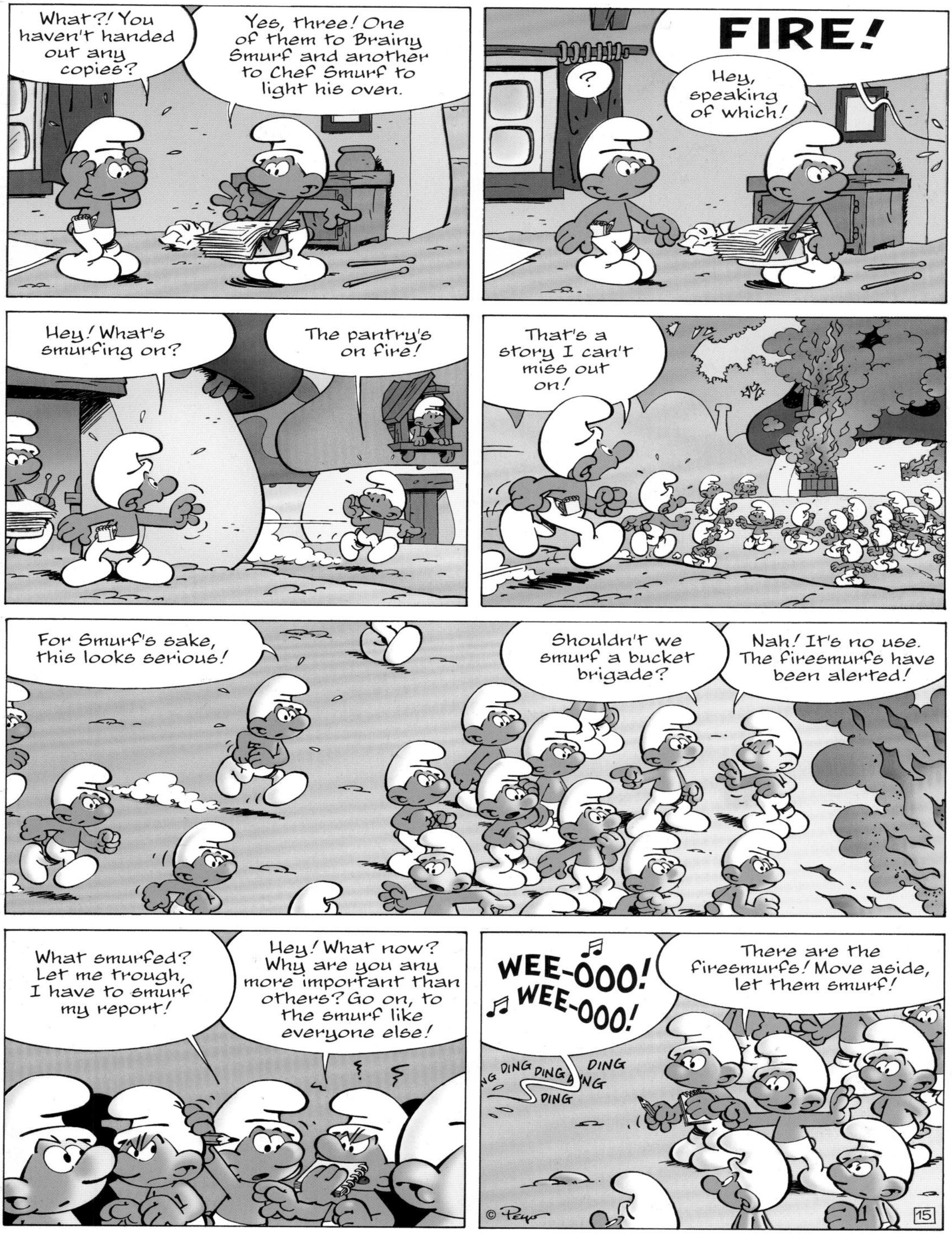
What?! You haven't handed out any copies?
Yes, three! One of them to Brainy Smurf and another to Chef Smurf to light his oven.
?
FIRE!
Hey, speaking of which!
Hey! What's smurfing on?
The pantry's on fire!
That's a story I can't miss out on!
For Smurf's sake, this looks serious!
Shouldn't we smurf a bucket brigade?
Nah! It's no use. The firesmurfs have been alerted!
What smurfed? Let me trough, I have to smurf my report!
Hey! What now? Why are you any more important than others? Go on, to the smurf like everyone else!
WEE-OOO! WEE-OOO!
DING DING DING DING DING
There are the firesmurfs! Move aside, let them smurf!
© Peyo
15

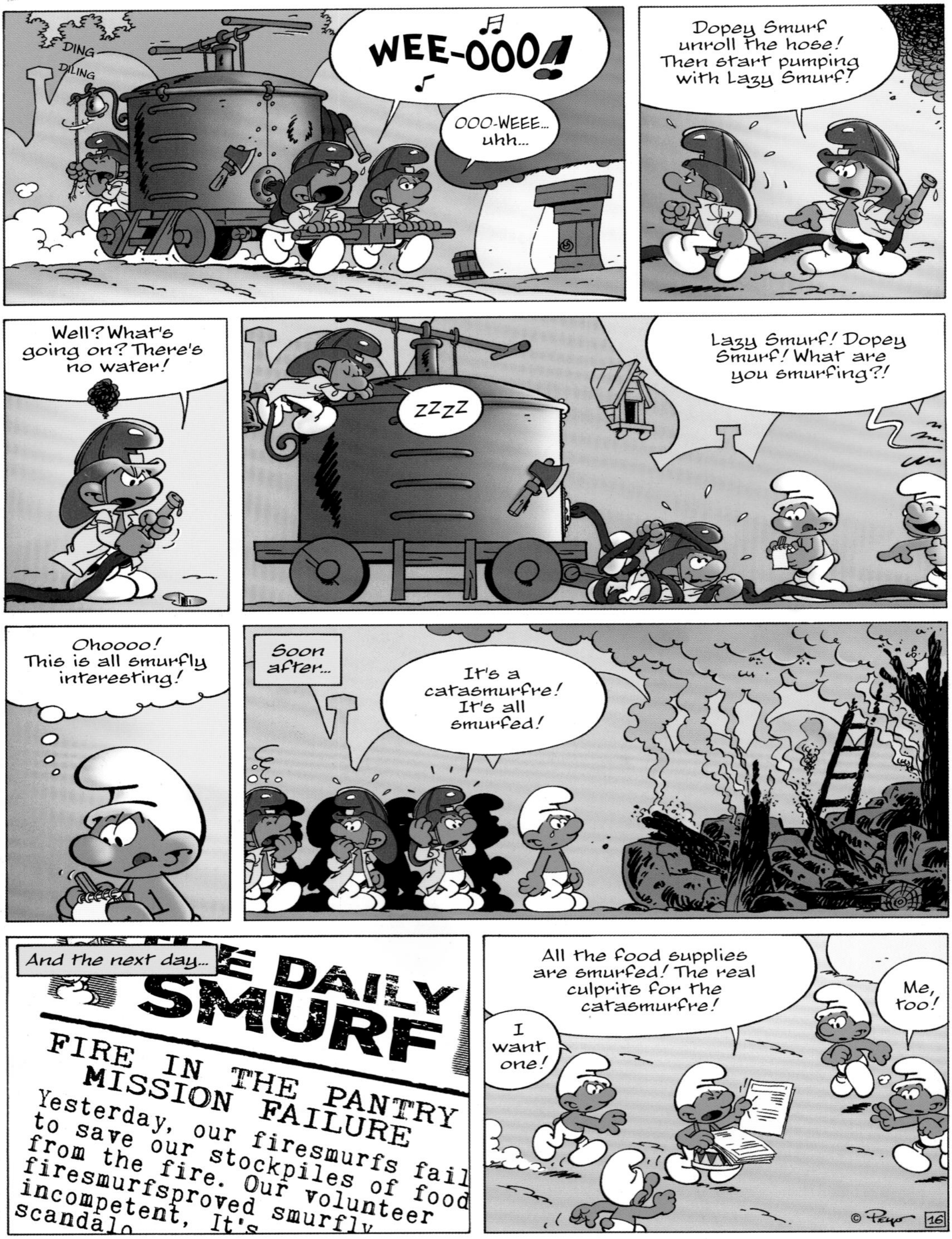
DING
DILING
WEE-OOO!
OOO-WEEE... uhh...
Dopey Smurf unroll the hose! Then start pumping with Lazy Smurf!
Well? What's going on? There's no water!
ZZZZ
Lazy Smurf! Dopey Smurf! What are you smurfing?!
Ohoooo! This is all smurfly interesting!
Soon after...
It's a catasmurfre! It's all smurfed!
And the next day...
E DAILY SMURF
FIRE IN THE PANTRY
MISSION FAILURE
Yesterday, our firesmurfs fail to save our stockpiles of food from the fire. Our volunteer firesmurfsproved incompetent, It's smurfly scandalo
All the food supplies are smurfed! The real culprits for the catasmurfre!
I want one!
Me, too!
© Peyo
16

Did you see that?! Lazy Smurf was sleeping while the pantry smurfed up in flames!

And Dopey Smurf--did you read that? Ha Ha! Ha! Good ol' Dopey Smurf!

Whoa! Unbelievable! Who'd have thought?

What?! They took all of them?

Every last one! Even my drum!

So, that's what we have to do! Controversies! Bombshell news!

And also find a way for me to be recognizable and be allowed to smurf everywhere! Hmm...

Later, at Tailor Smurf's...

What?! Could I smurf you a Reporter Smurf outfit? Obviously! I got exactly what you need!

Uh...I'm not sure this is appropriate.

How's that?

Nah!

No way! Out of the question!

Mmm...No! You're right, not this one either!

I'm out of ideas! That's the first time this has ever happened to me!

And what's that?

Bah! It's a defective model, it won't look good on you!

On the contrary, it's just what I need!

© Peyo 17

21

I can even smurf the press card I smurfed for myself on it!

Hey, at least smurf on a tie, you'll look more serious!

If you let those Smurfs do as they please, they'd dress any old way!

Now, to work! Let's go get a scoop!

Uh... that's all good and fine, but how do you smurf a scoop?

What are you talking about, Timber Smurf?

!

Come with me to the dam, you'll see the seriousness of the situation for yourself!

?

Hmmm, that's fishy! Let's follow them!

Later, at the dam...

See, the wood's rotten and is letting water smurf through! And there are several like that!

Hmm, yeah... In any case, I don't have time to take care of that! I have other smurfs to fry!

This will do fine for a bit longer!

Heh heh heh! This will surely interest my readers...

You're right! Anyhow I don't have time to deal with that now either!

Bah... And nobody will know a thing!

© Peyo

18

Special Edition! The village threatened by Handy Smurf and Timber Smurf's carelessness!

Hey, for once it's not me!

Hey!

Hey!

?!

Later...

You should be ashamed! This is a real scandal!

What'll I smurf? Now they all know!

But, Papa Smurf, I assure you that dam will hold--

SILENCE!

I know it's not serious! I've known for some time, but the Smurfs didn't need to find out! Now they're worried!

Okay, go on! I'll fix it all! Go home and make yourself scarce for a while!

Hey, look!

It's them!

BOOOO, ASSASSINS!

RUBBISH!

SELL-OUTS!

And to think I was the one smurfed him his press! See if I do that again!

Shut up and run!

23

The following days, the accusatory headlines continue...

WHO ARE THE SCAMMERS?

You'll surely recognize these thr individuals. What you don't know is while you were working dilige those three are scamming you by smurfing nothing to the...
One smurf

Lazy Smurf really could smurf a little more...

Yep! Or else he won't get any more of my veggies!

I think we should also force Jokey Smurf to stop his practical smurfs!

I was telling myself, too, this couldn't go on!

But a reporter's job is not without risk...

NOK NOK

Yes, what's that?

Reporter Smurf, I have a present for you!

BOOM

Hee hee hee! It's a present from Jokey Smurf!

The next morning...

THE DAILY SMURF

A BOMBING!

Yesterday, our reporter was the victim of a coercive attack attempting to silence him! But be assured, your favorite newspaper won't smurf to the terrorist threat and will continue to denounce injustice and sla...

Our reporter, Joke Smurf's victim

The newspaper has now become a major part in the life of the Smurfs...

Hey, that's the way to go smurf at the dam!

© Peyo

Some of them have it delivered at home...

What are they smurfing? They're late delivering the newspaper!

20

24

Here's your news-paper!

WAP

The newspaper is soon enhanced with many new columns, including: horoscopes...

"Smurfs born under the Taurus sign: Beware of falling objects!" >Pfff,< I don't believe a word of that!

You're wrong!

Besides, all we Smurfs know is that we were born one night when the moon was blue! So, how do we know who's a Taurus and who isn't?

Yeah, that's true!

BONK

Ah! You must be a Taurus!

Smurfette's romance novels...

...And the princess watched her prince smurf ride away on his faithful steed into the sunset with no hope of returning... The End!

I wonder who smurfs this nonsense?!

?!

BWAAAAH! The poor princess! You're heartless, Hefty Smurf!

HONK

© Peyo

21

25

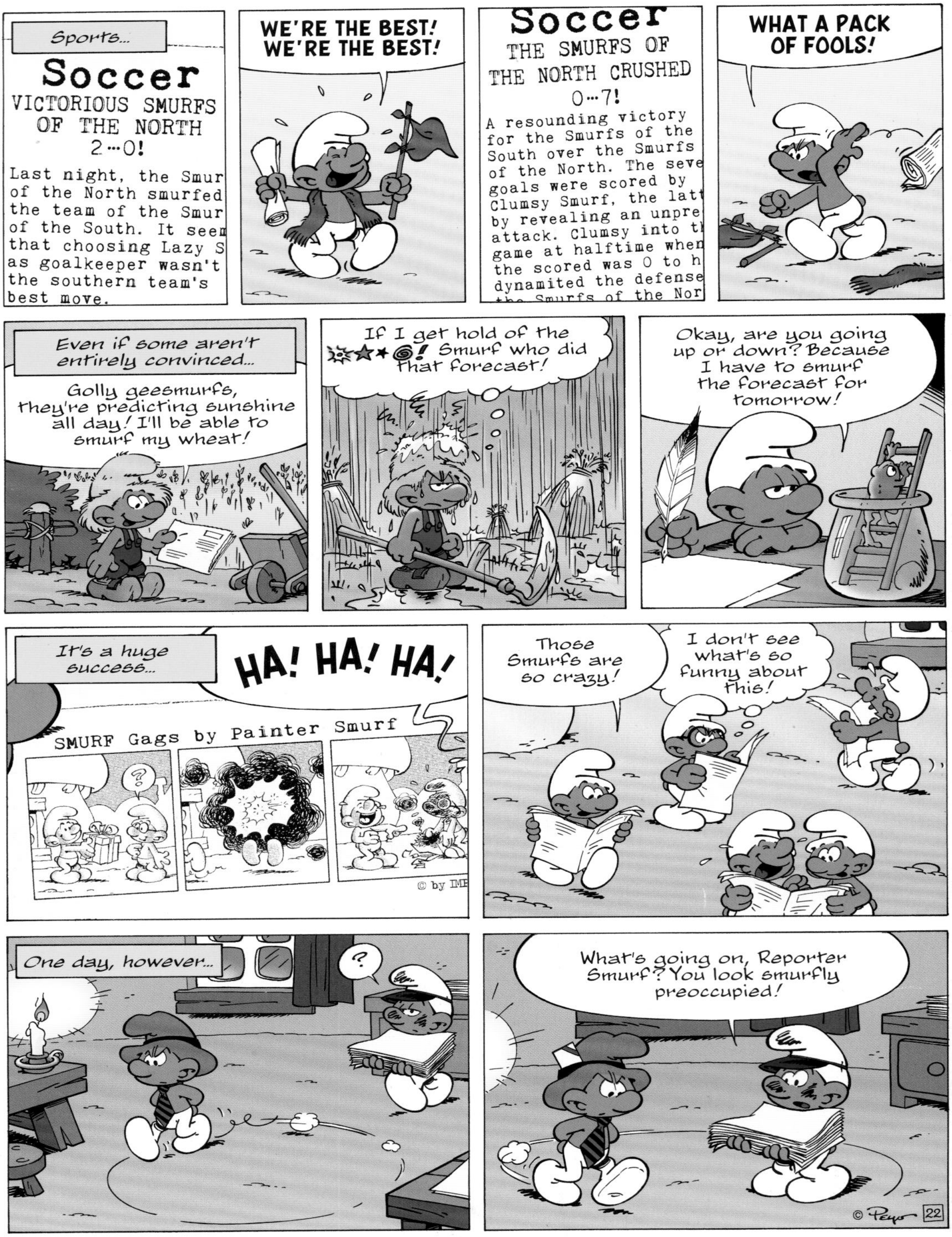
Sports...
Soccer
VICTORIOUS SMURFS OF THE NORTH 2...0!
Last night, the Smur of the North smurfed the team of the Smur of the South. It seem that choosing Lazy S as goalkeeper wasn't the southern team's best move.
WE'RE THE BEST! WE'RE THE BEST!
Soccer
THE SMURFS OF THE NORTH CRUSHED 0...7!
A resounding victory for the Smurfs of the South over the Smurfs of the North. The seve goals were scored by Clumsy Smurf, the latt by revealing an unpre attack. Clumsy into t game at halftime when the scored was 0 to h dynamited the defense
WHAT A PACK OF FOOLS!
Even if some aren't entirely convinced...
Golly geesmurfs, they're predicting sunshine all day! I'll be able to smurf my wheat!
If I get hold of the ☼★✶@! Smurf who did that forecast!
Okay, are you going up or down? Because I have to smurf the forecast for tomorrow!
It's a huge success...
HA! HA! HA!
SMURF Gags by Painter Smurf
?
© by IMP
Those Smurfs are so crazy!
I don't see what's so funny about this!
One day, however...
?
What's going on, Reporter Smurf? You look smurfly preoccupied!
© Peyo 22

But everything's fine! Every Smurf reads your newspaper now and waits impatiently for the daily news!

That's just it, I don't have the slightest news or the tiniest, little scandal for tomorrow! Nothing!

It's a catasmurfre! Something must be smurfed! The newspaper must come out, or else it's the end...

Talk about security problems in the village...

Done!

Greedy Smurf, who smurfs twice as much as the others...

Caterpillars smurfing all the sarsaparilla!

That, too!

You idiot, you're Greedy Smurf!

Uhh... Reporter Smurf?

I've finished my new story for the newspaper! Could you read it over?

Of course, Smurfette!

Excuse me for not staying, but I'm so tired! I'm going to smurf to bed!

Goodnight!

Goodnight, Smurfette!

Aah... Smurfette! I wonder who she's in love with--

Me too! I'd smurf dearly to find out!

!

27

WHY YES, OF COURSE! THERE'S THE IDEA!

SMACK

Thank you, Greedy Smurf!

But... what's the idea?

You'll see tomorrow, in the newspaper!

The next morning...

THE DAILY SMURF

SMURFETTE IS IN LOVE...

BUT WITH WHOM?

Her heart beats secretly for a Smurf. Even though she fiercely denies it, she's surely dreams of a Smurf Charming. But who's th... THE SMURFS HAVE THE ...HT TO KNOW THE...

I wonder who it could be? I'd have a word or two to smurf to him!

Uh...I promise you it's not me, Hefty Smurf?!

WAP WAP

Hey! Hey! I knew it! The Smurfs are snapping up today's edition!

Yes, but...I don't understand! You don't say who she's in love with in your newspaper!

Exactly! That's what so ingenious! You ask the question, but you never answer it!

Really? That's ingenious?!

Why, yes, of course! If you answer the question, nobody'll be interested anymore! On the other hand, if you don't answer it, the Smurfs will want to know the answer and will, therefore, continue to smurf the newspaper! You got it?

SCRTCH SCRTCH

No! But anyhow, we're going to get the answer! I see Smurfette smurfing this way!

© Peyo 24

Uh...can you meet with her? I have an important article to smurf!

?

28

Who's responsible for this pack of lies?

He had to step out. May I smurf him a message?

GLADLY!

SMACK

Tell him he shouldn't be talking about my private life in his rag!

And he can no longer count on me to smurf my novel.

Unfortunately for Smurfette, this was only the beginning of a long ordeal...

Ma-a-a-gnificent! You're magnificent, Smurfette!

You'll be superb for the opening of the Full Moon Ball! I'm quite proud of my work!

I'm impatient to see how many heads it'll smurf! I'll have never been so beautiful!

© Peyo

25

What's wrong, Smurfette?

I thought I smurfed something! Like a noise...

Bah! It's probably my imagination smurfing tricks on me! But you can never be too careful!

-Whew!-

SLAM

Ohooo, that's a scoop that'll generate some buzz!

Later...

Is that understood, Tailor Smurf? Not a peep about that new dress, or else I change designers!

Promise!

Tee hee hee! What a marvelous surprise I'll smurf them!

Hello, Handy Smurf!

Hello, Smurfette, I'm impatient to see it!

?! "Impatient to see it"... !?! I wonder what he smurfed by that...

Very nice choice with little blue flowers, Smurfette! I can't wait to be there!

?

© Peyo

26

What's up with all of you with your mysterious phrases? What are you talking about?

About your dress they're talking about it in the newspaper, Smurfette! All the Smurfs know about it! You'll be the prettiest one once again! I'm smurfly jealous!

THE DAILY SMURF
EXCLUSIVE!
SMURFETTE'S DRESS FOR THE

But...But...

Smurfette, such a smurfiful dress! Why?!

Aaah, what character! Now, that's a Smurfette!

Soon after...

Reporter Smurf, may I speak with you for a few moments?!

?

I've heard you've been harassing Smurfette! You know, being a reporter requires a certain code of ethics, meaning a certain morality! You mustn't just smurf any old thing!

But, Papa Smurf, my readers are the ones who want to--

That's no excuse!

I'm ordering you to stop smurfing Smurfette with this foolishness! Is that understood?!

In the end, it's not complicated being Papa Smurf! You let them smurf their thing and when they go off track, you get mad and everything returns to normal!

© Peyo 27

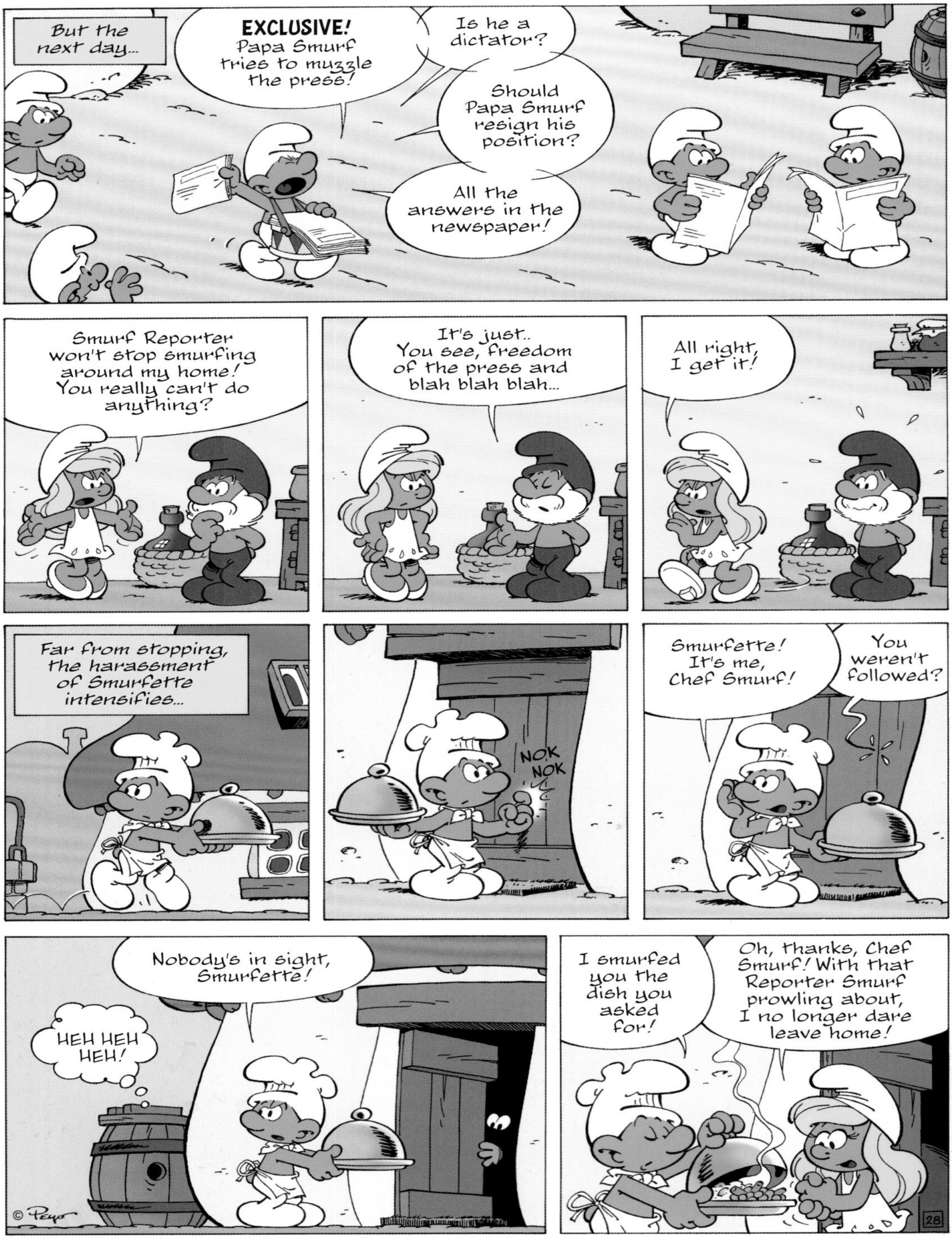
But the next day...
EXCLUSIVE! Papa Smurf tries to muzzle the press!
Is he a dictator?
Should Papa Smurf resign his position?
All the answers in the newspaper!
Smurf Reporter won't stop smurfing around my home! You really can't do anything?
It's just.. You see, freedom of the press and blah blah blah...
All right, I get it!
Far from stopping, the harassment of Smurfette intensifies...
NOK NOK
Smurfette! It's me, Chef Smurf!
You weren't followed?
Nobody's in sight, Smurfette!
HEH HEH HEH!
I smurfed you the dish you asked for!
Oh, thanks, Chef Smurf! With that Reporter Smurf prowling about, I no longer dare leave home!
© Peyo
28

You're a sweetheart!

SMACK

Ohooo! Did you see that?

?

See you tomorrow!

G...

That Chef Smurf ought to be more careful! He's working too much!

?

Peyew! This trash smurfs really bad! Hup, here it goes in the trashcan!

!

Yuck!

Soon after, at the press...

Don't make faces, Greedy Smurf! A real reporter's got to smurf a scoop no matter what the cost!

And this one will get Smurfs talking!

RUB RUB

Indeed...

THE D SMU

IS CHEF SMURF SMURFETTE'S HIDDEN LOVE?

She kissed him! Are they in love? Will he be her date to the ball?

Chef Smurf was seen ...er, smurfing in secret to ...cculent little dish, nice ...beknown...

Don't you think the food hasn't been the same for some time now?

You're smurfly right! Like some little taste of I don't know what!

I wonder if we shouldn't look for another chef!

?!

© Peyo

And come the night of the Full Moon Ball...

I bet we won't see Smurfette this evening! She hasn't poked her head out her door in three days!

You lose! There she is!

You see that? She came without her dress!

And no date!

Good evening, Smurfette! Hey, you didn't wear your new dress? And Chef Smurf didn't come with you?

Uh... did... did I say something wrong...?! It... It was in the newspaper, so...

BUHWAAH!

?   !   ?

Smurfette, what's going on?

≥Sniff,≤ ≥sniff,≤ ≥boohoo≤...

Come now, you mustn't smurf like that!

What's wrong?

© Peyo

30

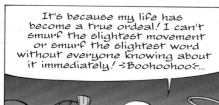
It's because my life has become a true ordeal! I can't smurf the slightest movement or smurf the slightest word without everyone knowing about it immediately! ÷Boohoohoo÷...

I'm forced to stay smurfed up at home! And all because you won't stop reading that stupid newspaper that tells fake news about my private life!

Boohoooo... I'm so unhappy!

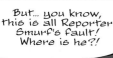

But... you know, this is all Reporter Smurf's fault! Where is he?!

Heh heh! Umm... Hey, you're here, Smurfette? This sarsaparilla juice is excellent... Heh heh!

A few days later...

?

Well, Reporter Smurf, is something wrong?

?

Ohh! Ever since the Smurfs decided to no longer smurf Smurfette any trouble, nobody's reading the newspaper anymore!

Your mistake was forgetting why you wanted to create a newspaper!

© Peyo

A true reporter's role is to smurf the facts as objectively as possible! He must smurf the public and warn them against all the dangers threatening them...

31

Danger?

Hey! Wait! I'm not done!

Uh... I'll be back right away, Papa Smurf!

Why didn't I smurf of that sooner?

Later, at nightfall...

Heh heh heh! A great reporter always lands on his smurfs!

What Smurf wouldn't be interested in a report on his greatest enemy: Gargamel?!

Nobody in sight! He's probably smurfing in the forest up to no good...

→Gulp!←... Courage! The survival of "The Daily Smurf" depends on it!

Boldness and discretion are the qualities a good reporter must smurf!

© Peyo

Here's an ideal vantage point! From here, I'll be able to spy on Gargamel with no fear of being smurfed!

32

I'd completely forgotten about him!

HA! HA! HA!

Stupid animal! BLUH BLUBLUHB!

BONG

Azrael slowly approaches the poor, defenseless Reporter Smurf...

33

STOP, YOU STUPID BEAST!

WAP

MRAW!

Luckily I got here in time! This Smurf is mine, do you hear? **MINE!**

Later...

My head! Where am I?

Why... why... I'm a prisoner!

?!

Yes! You are actually my prisoner! Heh heh heh!

GARGAMEL!

Say, you have funny clothes for a Smurf! Who are you?

I'm the Reporter Smurf!

The Reporter Smurf?! What's that?

Carried away by his passion, the Reporter Smurf told Gargamel his story...

© Peyo

And the Smurfs believe everything you tell them in your newspaper?!

WHY OF COURSE!

34

It's unbelievable what those Smurfs come up with! But that gives me an incredibly devious idea! Heh heh heh!

What are you going to smurf to me, you dirty wizard?

We'll see about that later! In any case, your fate is sealed, like that of the other Smurfs!

What do you mean?

Simply that I'm preparing a potion that'll allow me to find the way to your village without ever needing one of you to guide me there again!

Tomorrow, it'll be ready, and I'll finally be able to capture all the Smurfs and wreak my vengeance!

Obviously, if someone were to come throw a leaf of sarsaparilla in my mixture, it would be irreparably ruined!

But who would get such an idea? Nobody knows about it!

!

⇒YAWN!⇐ I'm going to bed! Tomorrow's an important day! I have to be in good condition!

Later, in the middle of the night...

⇒Sniff!⇐ Knowing a great threat is hanging over the village, and I'm not there to cover the event!

If I could at least--?! But... but that's--

35

THE KEY! That idiot Gargamel forgot it! He's even stupider than we thought!

39

A few moments later...

Quick! I must warn the Smurfs to keep him from smurfing his potion!

MRAW! FSCHHHH!

Quiet, Azrael, quiet...

Let the naïve, little thing run! Soon a lot more will come back and stumble right into my trap!

Come, let's prepare a surprise for them with this excellent glue I've been busy making.

After a long run, the Reporter Smurf arrives at the Smurfs Village...

Quick, I'll smurf a special edition!

Oh! Well, the old methods still have some good in them, after all...

SMURF ALERT! EVERYBODY GET UP!

CLANG CLONG

?

Z

© Peyo

36

Hey! Reporter Smurf? Have you fallen on your smurf or what?! It's past midnight!

Wake up, the village is in danger! Gargamel's making a plan to smurf us!

What's this all about? Where did you come from?

The Reporter Smurf soon tells of his misadventure...

Well, that's nothing to be proud of, Reporter Smurf. Your taste for sensationalism has made you smurf some foolish risks!

As for that so-called potion, I don't believe it! No such spell exists! He's smurfed one over on you!

You were lucky to escape him! I hope that will smurf you a lesson!

All right, all of you back to bed now! It's late, good night!

Well, I know what I saw and heard! He even said a sarsaparilla leaf would smurf his potion! That's proof, isn't it?!

37

Obviously, if he said that...

Oh, yes, that sounds serious...

Say, Reporter Smurf, would you have smurfed that news in your newspaper?

Of course, Hefty Smurf!

Then, it's true because, if it's in the newspaper, it must be true!

Yes, but Papa Smurf said--

Bah! Papa Smurf's getting old!

Yes, and remember that he already tried to censor my newspaper...

All right, everyone to Gargamel's! We have to smurf his plan!

Let's not forget a sarsaparilla leaf!

Later...

⇨Gulp!⇦ I'm sure we're smurfing straight into trouble...

Wimp!

If you don't smurf up, you'll be the one having trouble!

!

Come on! Smurf with me! ⇨HMMPF!⇦

CREEEE

Nobody in sight! Gargamel and his stupid cat must sleep like logs...

I have my own private entrance from which I can smurf my report for tomorrow's edition...

© Peyo

38

42

Come on, smurf silently after me...

I'd like to see his face tomorrow, once he sees his mixture's been smurfed...

?

Hey?! What's this smurf?!

Why... This smurf is sticky! Help me, I'm smurfed!

Us, too!

!?

Ha! Ha! Ha! Who's that? Why it's the Smurfs! Look, Azrael, they're like common, trapped flies! That strong glue is excellent, isn't it, my friends?

GARGAMEL!

I told you we shouldn't have smurfed here!

It was a trap! It's all my fault, I'm the one who led them here!

It's a catasmurfre! They're going to get smurfed!

39

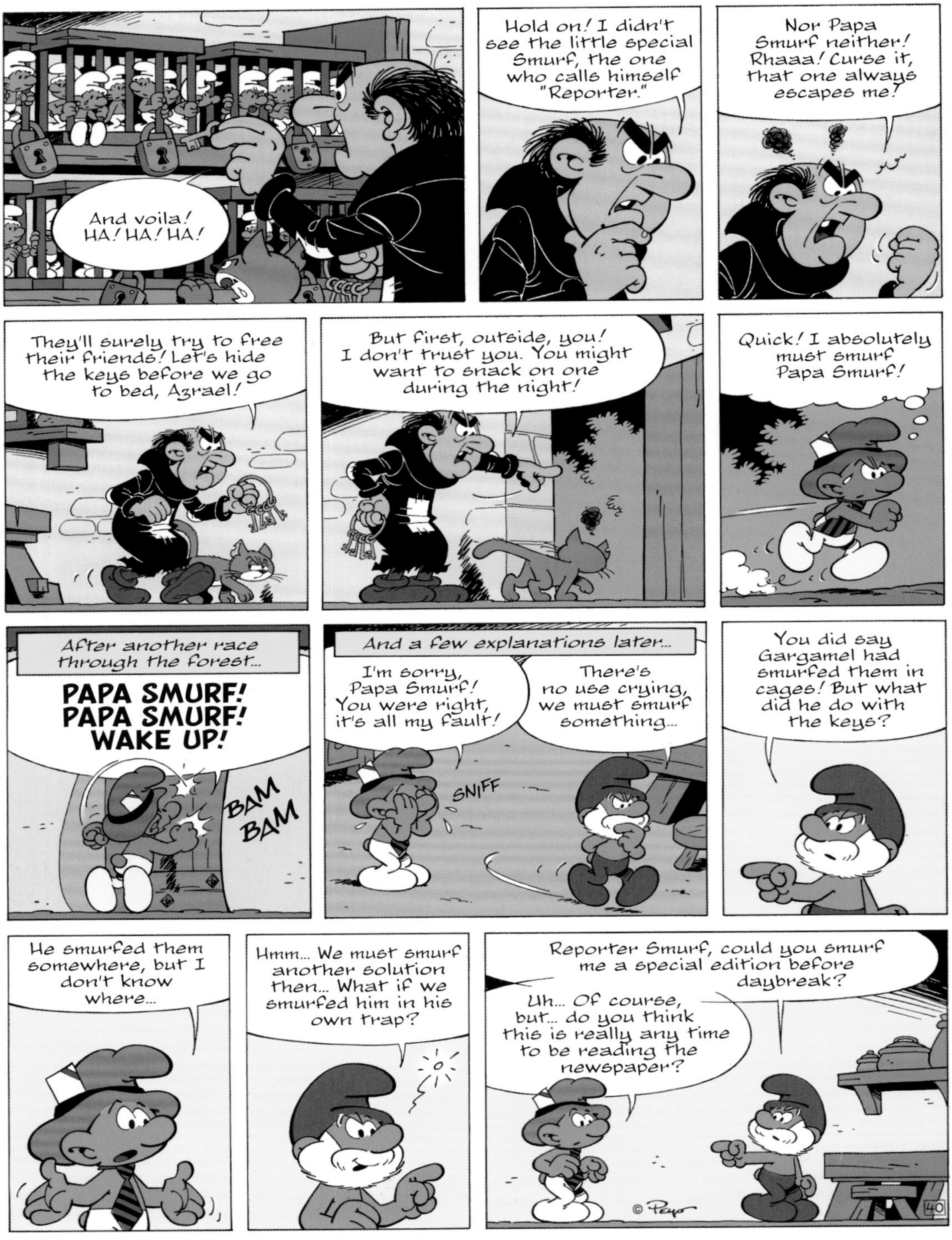
And voila!
HA! HA! HA!
Hold on! I didn't see the little special Smurf, the one who calls himself "Reporter."
Nor Papa Smurf neither! Rhaaa! Curse it, that one always escapes me!
They'll surely try to free their friends! Let's hide the keys before we go to bed, Azrael!
But first, outside, you! I don't trust you. You might want to snack on one during the night!
Quick! I absolutely must smurf Papa Smurf!
After another race through the forest...
PAPA SMURF! PAPA SMURF! WAKE UP!
BAM BAM
And a few explanations later...
I'm sorry, Papa Smurf! You were right, it's all my fault!
SNIFF
There's no use crying, we must smurf something...
You did say Gargamel had smurfed them in cages! But what did he do with the keys?
He smurfed them somewhere, but I don't know where...
Hmm... We must smurf another solution then... What if we smurfed him in his own trap?
Reporter Smurf, could you smurf me a special edition before daybreak?
Uh... Of course, but... do you think this is really any time to be reading the newspaper?
© Peyo
40

I'll explain to you at the press! Quick, we only have a little time to act!

?

The special edition soon came off the press...

Perfect, Reporter Smurf! That's exactly what I needed! Now, it's our turn to trap Gargamel!

And later...

We'll have to be quick! The sun's coming up!

You know what you must smurf! I'll see to Gargamel, and watch out for Azrael!

There's no danger. Gargamel smurfed him out of the house...

The Reporter Smurf! He came back to rescue us!

Shh! I don't have the keys, but Papa Smurf has a plan!

What are you going to smurf'?

It's part of the plan! Don't worry, it's just a bit of color...

SLURP

!?

HEY!

PFFFFFRT

Soon after...

It's done, Papa Smurf! I also smurfed them the instructions!

Perfect! Let's hurry and go, the sun's up!

Too bad, I'd smurf dearly to be here and see the face Gargamel makes...

Hee hee hee!

© Peyo

41

45

COCKADOODLE-DOO

AAAH!

So, let's go see our little blue boarders... ?

!

"The Smurfs stricken with the same illness!" What kind of story is this?

THE DAILY SMURF

THE SMURFS STRICKEN WITH THE SAME ILLNESS

"It seems a bad virus has affected the Smurfs. While it's not dangerous for them... with a vague sluggishness and eruption of temporary bumps...it is, however, extremely dangerous for humans who should avoid all contact with infected Smurfs, or else they risk being smurfed into filthy toads full of boils..."

This must be the newspaper of that blasted Reporter Smurf! He's trying to fool me, but the trap is too crude! HA! HA! HA!

Did you hear, you little vermin? It seems you're si— ?!!

WHAT?! What's wrong with you?

→Buuuuh←... I don't know, it's like I have a smurf here, on my stomach..

I can't even smurf my arm anymore...

You too! What's wrong with you?

© Peyo

42

What do you mean what's wrong with me? Why are you looking at me like that?

Quick! A mirror!

AAAH!

It's horrible! I'm disfigured!

⇒Pffrrt!⇐ Hee hee!

Rhaaa! I'm sure it's a trap!

Yes, but what if it were true?!

CROAK

"The only remedy is a quick quarantine in the hour following contamination, before the transformation becomes irreversible!"

QUICK!

I hope it's not too late...

Go! Leave! Go home, you dirty, little plague-bearers!

HEE HEE HEE! That idiot Gargamel smurfed the whole story! Thanks, Papa Smurf! Well done, Reporter Smurf!

Quick, back to the village!

43

÷Waaa!÷ For once I had all of them!

SNIF

!?

Why... why... what's this?! My boils are going away!

Paint and make-up! I got tricked again! You cursed Smurfs! I'll get revenge!

A few days later...

Ah! The Reporter Smurf! How's it smurfing?

It's smurfing fine, Papa Smurf! But, you know, you mustn't call me that anymore!

That's true, I heard you decided not to smurf your newspaper anymore!

Well, you know, it was a good lesson for all of us! I think the Smurfs realized you mustn't believe everything you hear...

?

Hey, did you smurf the latest? It seems Brainy Smurf smurfed Hefty Smurf a thrashing...

No?

It would even seem he did so with a single hand, while reading a collection of fables with the other...

Wow! Incredible! Who'd have believed it?

Come on, don't mope! Smurfs are Smurfs, you have to give them time...

© Peyo

It's like with Lazy Smurf! You have to give him time to change, too! I heard that, recently, he'd smurfed in his bed for three days without waking up... Well... That's what I heard... Hmm! Uh... What were we just smurfing about?

!

THE END

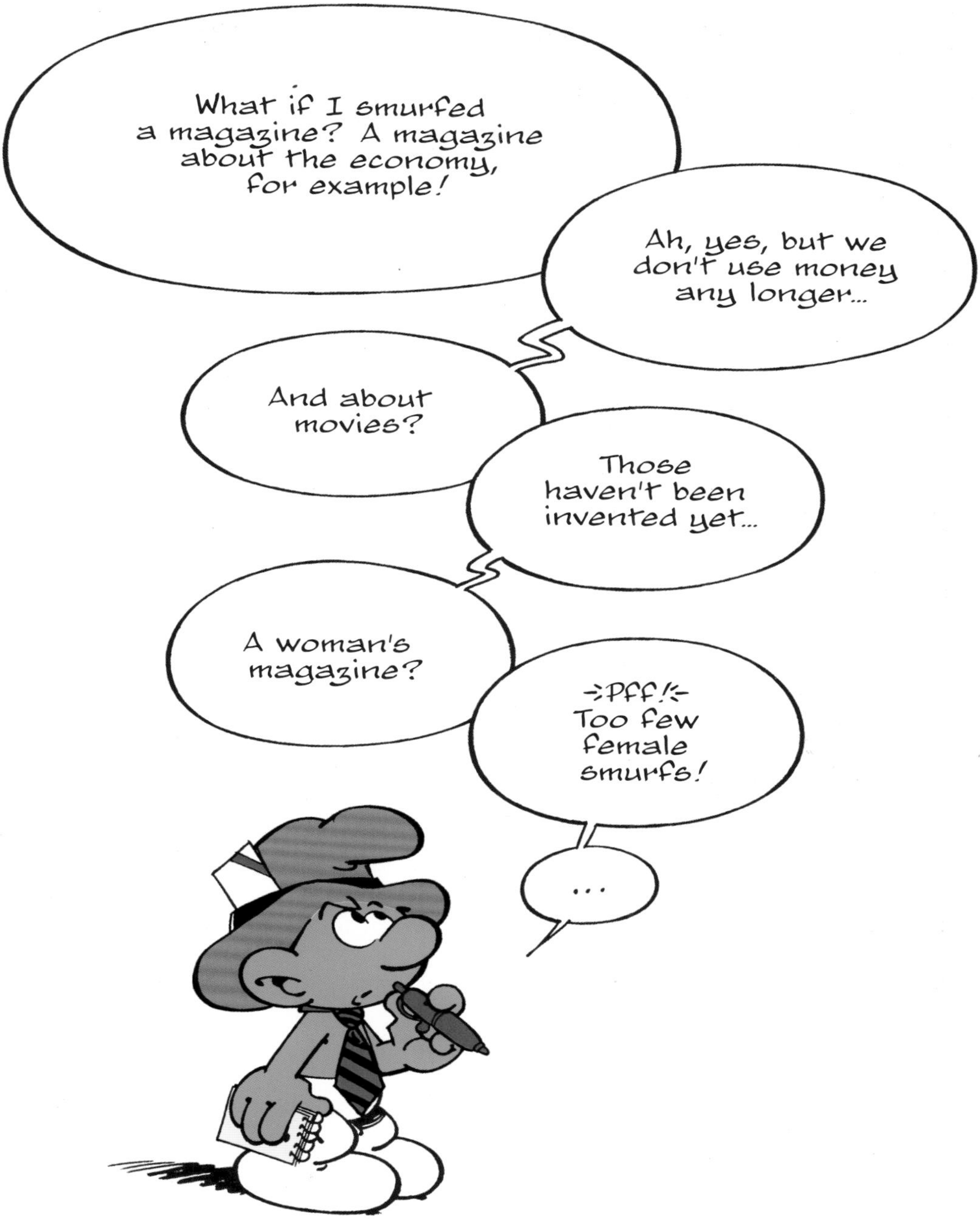
What if I smurfed a magazine? A magazine about the economy, for example!
Ah, yes, but we don't use money any longer...
And about movies?
Those haven't been invented yet...
A woman's magazine?
Pff! Too few female smurfs!
...

WATCH OUT FOR PAPERCUTZ™

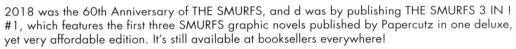

W elcome to the totally-timely twenty-fourth SMURFS graphic novel by Peyo, from Papercutz, those diligent believers in the freedom of the Press who are dedicated to publishing great graphic novels for all ages. I'm Jim Salicrup, your mild-mannered Smurf-in-Chief, here to make a couple of BIG ANNOUNCEMENTS!

2018 was the 60th Anniversary of THE SMURFS, and d was by publishing THE SMURFS 3 IN ! #1, which features the first three SMURFS graphic novels published by Papercutz in one deluxe, yet very affordable edition. It's still available at booksellers everywhere!

Within the pages of THE SMURFS 3-IN-1 #1, you'll find the story in which the Smurfs made their historic debut—a Johan and Peewit adventure entitled "The Smurfs and the Magic Flute." As a special treat for you here, we're publishing a special anniversary story that's a sequel to the very first SMURFS story, on the following pages. The story, just like the Smurf's Anniversary, continues in our next SMURFS graphic novel THE SMURFS #25 "The Gambling Smurfs" coming soon.

Now, a few words about "The Smurf Reporter," even though this story was originally published 15 years ago, it's as relevant today, as it was then. The press needs to be free to tell the truth, and that means no "Fake News." Both the government and the press need to keep each other in check, for, as great comics writer and editor Stan Lee once wrote, "with great power, must also come great responsibility."

We asked co-writer Luc Parthoens a few questions about how this story came to be and present that in on the following pages.

Finally, on behalf of everyone at Papercutz, may I express our eternal thanks to Pierre Culliford, better known as "Peyo," for creating THE SMURFS 60 years ago! And to the Smurfs themselves, Happy Smurfday!

Smurf you later,

Jim

STAY IN TOUCH!

EMAIL: salicrup@papercutz.com
WEB: papercutz.com
TWITTER: @papercutzgn
INSTAGRAM: @papercutzgn
FACEBOOK: PAPERCUTZGRAPHICNOVELS
FANMAIL: Papercutz, 160 Broadway, Suite 700, East Wing, New York, NY 10038

LUC PARTHOENS

While Pierre Culliford, better known as Peyo, is the creator of THE SMURFS, he has enlisted many talented writers and cartoonists over the years to join Studio Peyo to help him meet the ever-increasing demand for SMURFS comics. Since his death in 1992, his studio has completely taken over the creation of new comics featuring THE SMURFS, BENNY BREAKIRON, and JOHAN AND PEEWIT. One such creator, Luc Parthoens, has been playing a major role in contributing to those new comics, and we thought it would be enlightening and interesting to interview him for this volume of THE SMURFS, which features "The Smurf Reporter," which Luc co-wrote with Thierry Culliford.

Papercutz: *Tell us a little about yourself. Where and when were you born?*
Luc Parthoens: I was born October 2, 1964, in Bujumbura (Burundi), Africa.

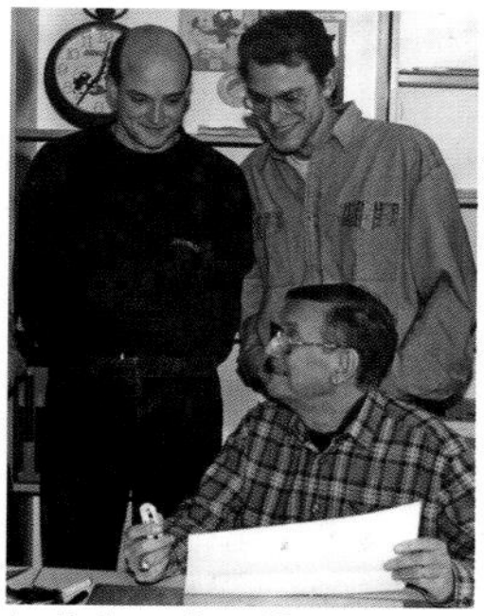
Luc Parthoens, Pascal Garray, and Peyo

Papercutz: *What did you want to do when you grew up?*
Luc: When I was a kid, I was a big fan of European comics and western movies. When I became a teen, I discovered American comicbooks from Marvel and the new generation of the European comic artists such as Moebius and Pratt. From that time on, I knew that I wanted to work in this industry.

Papercutz: *How did you first discover THE SMURFS?*
Luc: My father was also a big fan of European comics. When we lived in Africa, he brought from Europe *Spirou* and *Tintin,* the comics compilation magazines. And it was, of course, in *Spirou* magazine that I discovered our favorite little blue imps. If I remember correctly, it was "The Astrosmurf"...

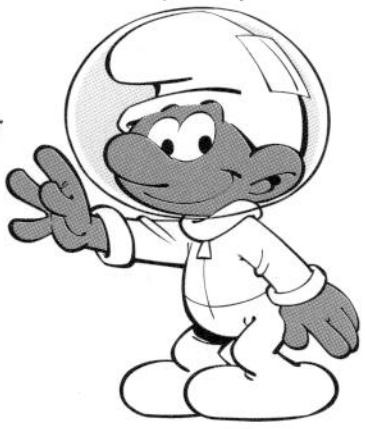

Papercutz: *Did you know Peyo?*
Luc: Yes, the first two years I worked for THE SMURFS, he was still alive. It was a great privilege to know him. He was an outstanding creator, a great narrator, and storyboarder.

Papercutz: *How did you wind up co-writing "The Smurf Reporter" with Thierry Culliford?*
Luc: I had written short comics (8-page stories) with Peyo for the SMURFS Magazine. After he died, by contract with a brand new publisher (Le Lombard), we had to start a new graphic novel. I had some scenarios and ideas that I proposed to Thierry Culliford. We started then a collaboration that lasted seven graphic novels. "The Smurf Reporter" was the fifth...

Papercutz: *What inspired the story?*
Luc: The trigger for the story of "The Smurf Reporter" was the polemic about the role of the paparazzi in the tragic accident of Lady Diana in Paris, a few years before. Thierry Culliford and I thought that it was an interesting start to show how a Smurf could have a good idea to serve the interest of the Smurf community by inventing journalism and became a paparazzi. And concerning the Smurf Reporter's look, our inspiration was Weegee, the American photographer.

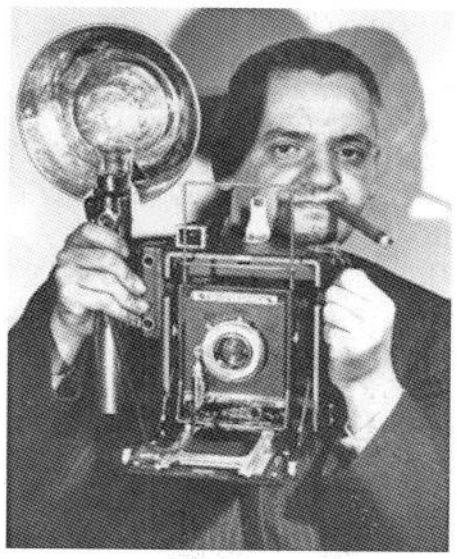
Weegee

Papercutz: *What do you do now with THE SMURFS?*
Luc: Now, I work on the scenarios of our new series of graphic novels "*Les Schtroumpfs et le village des filles*" [Look for THE SMURFS: THE VILLAGE BEHIND THE WALL #2 coming soon from Papercutz] that tells stories of the new Smurf girls characters from the last movie. I'm also on the team that works on our big project of a brand new 3D animated Smurfs TV series that will be on the screens for 2020! I'm really enthusiastic about it, it will be awesome!

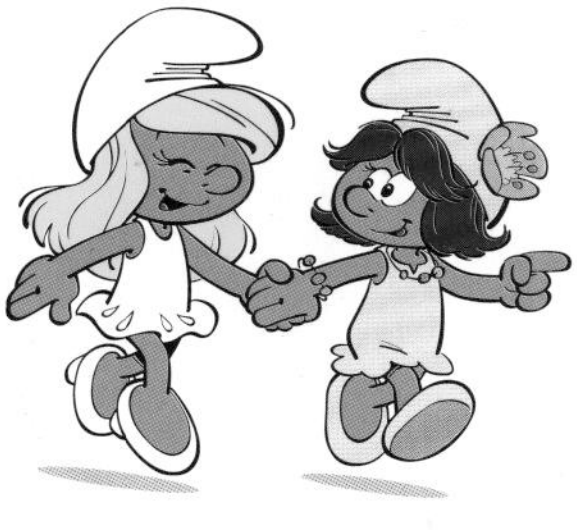

We thank Luc Parthoens for taking time out of his busy schedule to answer our questions.

THE FLUTE SMURFERS

Lazy Smurf, I'm just about smurfed up with you!

It's always the same with you! While others are smurfing, you're goofing off!

Papa Smurf said he wanted us to resmurf the roof of his laboratory before day's end!

≶YAWN!≶ All right, all right! We can still smurf a little nap, can't we?

HEY! LOOK OUT!

?

♪!

What are they smurfing up there?

Hey, you two, I asked you to **repaint** my laboratory, not to smurf it into pieces!

A stork has landed on your roof, Papa Smurf! It has a message smurfed to its foot!

A message?

My friend, the sorcerer Alderic, has written to me. He's asking me to smurf him a magic flute to cure one of his patients who's ill with a "Monotone Melancholy"!

It's been a long time since anyone smurfed such a request to us!

What's a "Monotone Melancholy," Papa Smurf?

It's an illness that smurfs humans especially! Those suffering from it are stricken with apathy! They go without smurfing the slightest movement all day long!

Like Lazy Smurf?

A little, yes! Except they don't sleep!

And only the sound of the flute has the power to bring them out of that condition!

Will you agree to smurf him the flute, Papa Smurf?

Of course!

YIPPEEEEE! We're going to smurf a flute!

That's cool!

Me, I don't like school!

Immediately, the Smurfs set out for the forest...

There, they carefully select the hundred-year-old oak tree with the heart from which they'll sculpt the flute...*

CHOP CHOP CHOP

Working tirelessly, little by little, the Smurfs carve the magical instrument...

3

*See THE SMURFS #2 "The Smurfs and the Magic Flute."

You've done good work, my little Smurfs! It's magnificent!

So, you three will accompany me among the humans! Go smurf your things. We're leaving immediately!

Later...

Say, Papa Smurf, why must we always stay hidden when we're among humans?

Only a few of them know of our existence, and it's better that it stay that way!

Because even if they're generally nice, some do have evil intentions! We'll have to smurf on our guard!

The trip continues over the Crystal Mountains and the Great Forest...

We're here! The house of my friend the sorcerer is smurfed in some woods just outside this village!

Let's hope he's home!

4

NOK
NOK

Papa Smurf! There you are! Come in!

I came as fast as I could!

Here's the flute! Be careful. You know it can be dangerous if misused!

Don't you worry, Papa Smurf! I'll finally be able to cure that unfortunate peasant!

What happened to the poor man?

About two weeks ago, he carelessly walked through a fairy ring! They say they're enchanted, you know!

A few days later, he fell ill. And since then, he stays in bed with a vacant gaze!

Even the village doctor could do nothing to bring him out of that state!

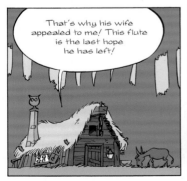

That's why his wife appealed to me! This flute is the last hope he has left!

But you could come with me to see the patient, Papa Smurf!

Gladly!

We'll wait for night to fall! It's best to be discreet, for one can be quickly accused of sorcery hereabouts!

5

56

Later...

There's their cottage!

I hope they won't scream when they see us!

I don't like it when humans scream. It really hurts your smurfs!

EEEEE!

Don't be afraid. The Smurfs are our friends! Here's their leader, Papa Smurf!

Delighted, madam! May I see the patient?

My poor husband!

Papa Smurf is a very competent physician!

Alas, I can only confirm your diagnosis! He is suffering from "Monotone Melancholy," and the sound of the flute is the only remedy!

6

What's going on in there? That's suspicious!

!?

Here, Alderic, the honor is yours.

Excuse me. Would everyone who's not a Smurf smurf... Stop up your ears!

What's that elf saying? That I have to stop up my--

What-- what's happening to me!?

Meanwhile, inside...

HEY?! OH!

STOP! Stop playing! That's enough!

Where am I? What happened to me?

You're cured!

PAPA!

He played the flute, and I couldn't keep myself from dancing! That's **WITCHCRAFT!**

And what's more, the peasant is cured when I failed to do so! ⸗RHAA⸗, I'm mad!

⸗Grrr⸗... It's thanks to that flute and those blue elves! But you won't get away with it, you old goat!

I have to come up with an idea to eliminate that old pest, or else I'm done for as a doctor in the area!

Thank you, Mister Papa Smurf, for restoring my Emile to me!

Thank Alderic instead! He's the one who asked us to make the flute!

Heh heh heh, I think I have an idea! But for that, **I'LL NEED THAT FLUTE!**

I knew the doctor wouldn't be able to cure you! His potions couldn't do anything against such an evil spell!

SMOOCH
SMOOCH

Now, if you'll excuse us, we must depart!

The sun will be up, and we best not be seen here! People might gossip!

8

Hey! Oh! Don't leave me here!

Careful, there they are!

And thanks again!

They're good folk!

Yes, even if the lady screams a little too loud!

For Smurf's sake! I forgot to smurf them one recommendation!

Wait here for me. I'll be back!

?

I'll follow them quietly! I'll surely find a moment to steal that flute from them!

!?

It's the elf who's carrying it on his back! AND ALONE! This is my chance!

What...? Who are you?

What are you-- ?! Help--

?

?

?!

BONK

60

Papa Smurf is in danger!

If someone smurfs a hair of his beard...

PAPA SMURF! Are you hurt?

Someone knocked me out!

And that dirty smurf fled on horseback!

OH, NO! It's a catasmurfphe!

What happened?

Alderic! A human stole the flute from me! We absolutely must smurf it!

He left on horseback that way!

A human? Well, I never! Who was it? Could you recognize him?

Alas, no! His face was hidden in the shadow! But he was tall with a big belly!

Uh, that's just not very precise, Papa Smurf! It won't be easy to find your thief!

Let's think! He fled towards the village. That's where we'll be able to find him again!

But you, Alderic, considering your reputation as a sorcerer, aren't welcome there!

Here's my idea! You'll drop us off near the village, we'll sneak in and try to unmask the thief! He won't be able to resist the temptation to use the flute!

Then we'll find a way to take it back from him! Let's go. There's not a moment to lose!

10

The next day...

WOOF! WOOF! GRRR...

By golly! Do you smell something, doggy?

?!?

What?! What sorcery is this?

Oo ☆

Hee hee hee! What a marvelous instrument!

BAAAAA BAAAA BAAAAA BAAAA BAAA ARF ARF

Now it's Old Man Frank's turn! His cows need a little dance number! Heh heh heh!

Soon, the villagers will be exasperated with all this witchcraft!

Then I'll just have to pin the responsibility on that old monkey of a sorcerer!

11

THE FLUTE SMURFER concludes in THE SMURFS #25 "The Gambling Smurfs," on sale soon.

PLAY the SMURFS' VILLAGE
MOBILE GAME FOR FREE!

© Peyo - 2019 - Licensed through Lafig Belgium - www.smurf.com

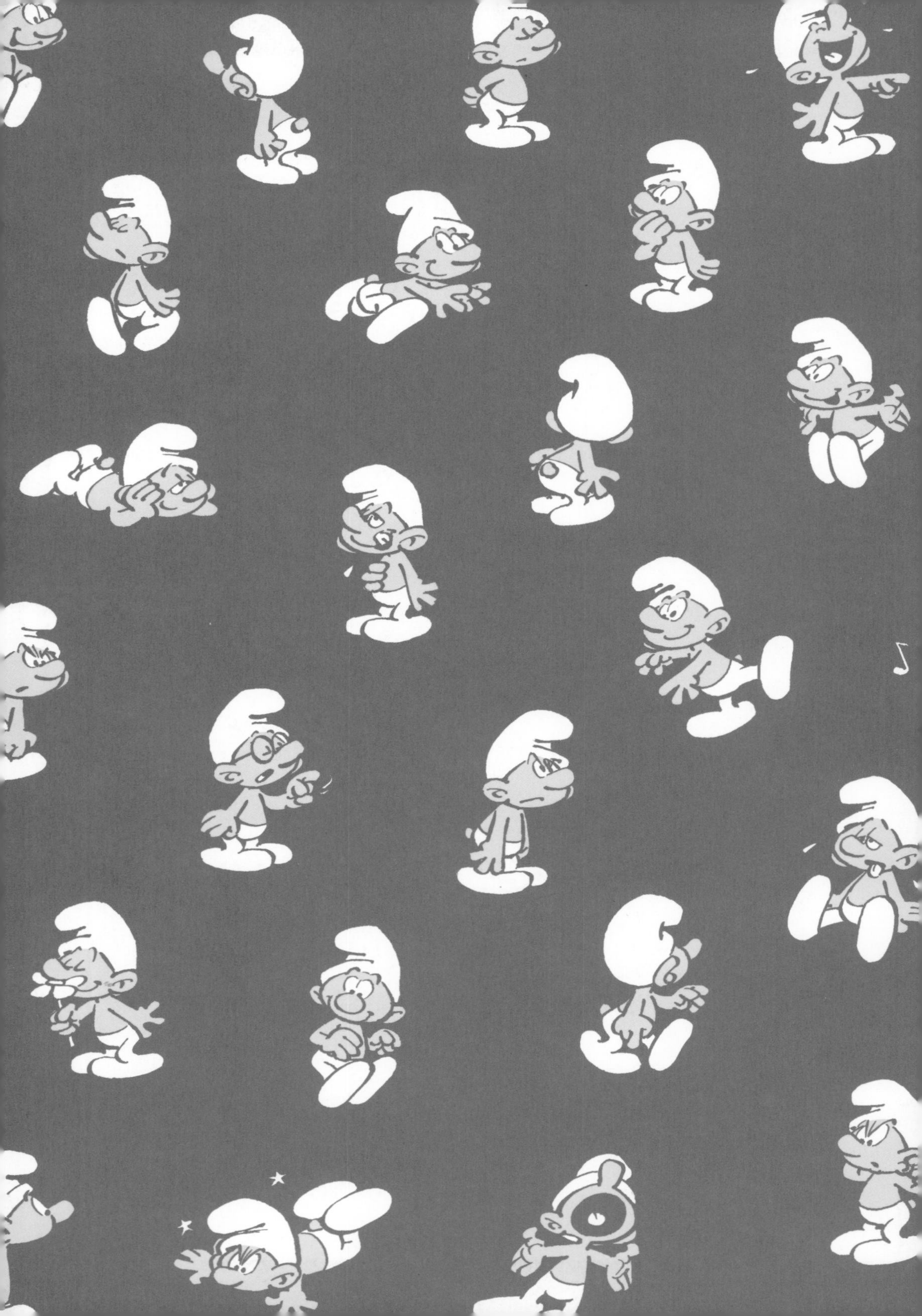